On the Future | In Stories
Volume 1: Megatrends

Short Stories

2nd revised edition (German), March 2016
Translated in English, unless the stories 'Last Celebration of the Meetings', 'Lilea's Reports', 'Healthy Flavours' by Samar Nahas (2016)

Authors: Sibylla Amstutz, Michael Doerk, Chris Ebbert, Urs Gaudenz, Julie Harboe, Ute Klotz, Barbara Kummler, Christine Larbig, Jens O. Meissner, Bettina Minder, Stijn Ossevoort, Roland Portmann, Christian Lars Schuchert, Ursula Sury, Patricia Wolf

Cover Photos: Konrad Marfurt

Herstellung & Verlag:BoD - Books on Demand, Norderstedt

ISBN 978-3-7431-9647-6

On the Future | In Stories

Foreword

Ute Klotz and Patricia Wolf

As educated and curious people, we are naturally fascinated by the future. At its best, our curiosity compels us to learn more about it. At its worst, it fuels our desire to change it today. Both don't work. The future in the present is still a grey blur – we can't foresee it. Not even a fortune teller can help us clear the fog from the crystal ball.

What we can do, however, is to imagine what it could be like, not in a deterministic manner but instead through stories. Exploring the future in this personal and proactive way spawns a variety of perspectives and interpretations of trends and topics. And mankind needs a plurality of stories also to counterbalance the conformism taking place in many aspects of our lives.

The stories in this book were written by the members of CreaLab, the future lab of the Lucerne University of Applied Sciences and Arts. They each relate to three megatrends from the Megatrend Map 2.0 of the Zukunftsinstitut in Vienna. The combination of trends and the stories that have emerged from them are unique. They are not predictions and are completely imaginary. And should they inspire readers for more stories about the future, we look forward to hearing from them at crealab@hslu.ch

.

Table of Contents

On the Future | In Stories

THE HAPPINESS OF COWS

TRENDS: URBAN FARMING, SUSTAINABILITY SOCIETY, DISTRICTS

BETTINA MINDER AND SIBYLLA AMSTUTZ

Interview with Jens Jan Jackobson, Cow-Working Coach (CWC), 19.02.2047

So now you're giving these cows life coaching. How did this come about?

Two developments became apparent to us in the past. The first was that our cows here in Switzerland were suffering from a major existential crisis. This became evident when the cows began to make dance moves and have laughing fits. Something utterly strange. We really were quite concerned about the mental health of our cows. The second development was that the farmers were at a loss and completely overwhelmed with how to deal with the heat stress these cows were experiencing. Traditional care and support concepts had entirely failed in this case. Due to this development, we began to experiment with different methods, such as cultural exchange, movement therapy, and new environments.

The model you developed is unique and has been very successful all over the world. Your cows are invited to congresses. What distinguishes this model?

The cows are given personal and meaningful tasks that are tailored to their specific needs, tasks such as traffic reduction and patient care. Every single cow differs in its abilities and personality traits. And that's why it's important to define these tasks together with each one of them. Our experience has shown that it is counterproductive to simply assign them tasks. For example, some cows are more adventurous and like to be on the move, whilst others prefer to remain in a familiar environment.

These tasks give the cows a sense of purpose. You can see that they take responsibility and become a part of society. In addition, with the cows we were able to establish new health models in the cities and districts. There are district cows that assist with transporting the shopping, and there are petting cows in selected communities that are also accessible to seniors. Furthermore, the cows are ubiquitous on our streets and, as a result, traffic has been reduced and the roads are much safer now.

And the second key element is our cultural exchange with India. We discovered that the cows, and in particular those in responsible positions, need time off to gain different impressions and gather new experiences. After the exchange in Delhi, many cows are more open for new tasks and can transfer their knowledge. Indian cows that live here bring a new culture to the West and in particular a sense of calm and serenity.

What does the urban population think about cows wandering around in public parks and on the streets?

It was certainly unusual and partly dangerous at first, as both humans and animals were unfamiliar with this sort of interaction. Apart from two or three unresolved issues, the model is now quite established here. People see the benefits and children especially have helped show adults these benefits. For example, children stuck in a traffic jam would step out of the car and go off to stroke the cows.

After a pilot phase, initially sceptical politicians finally acknowledged the financial and social added value of this model. The cows have now become such a natural part of our society that we can no longer imagine life without them.

What advice would you give to another country wishing to introduce this same model?

The effort involved in assessing and defining the cows' needs is not to be underestimated. That's something we learned. It pays to invest a lot of time at the beginning. Among other things, we conducted observational studies and then led several long sessions to discuss the results with the cows. During these sessions, the farmers, who at first were rather sceptical, helped us gain a better understanding of the cows. Amazingly, every single cow shared with us clearly what she wants and what she doesn't want. And that's how we generated a profile for every single cow. The data are saved in an interactive database, which allows us to match the requirements with the corresponding cow. It has worked really well so far.

In addition, we invited different categories of people, such as children, car drivers, caregiving institutions, the police, and senior citizens, to participate in the model. We profited tremendously from the elderly who had had childhood experiences with cows.

It's very important to maintain a cultural exchange with other countries that have already gathered experiences. We consider the cooperation with India an important aspect of this model. In the meantime, the cow-working community has grown rapidly worldwide, with annual events and a very active online exchange

Do you feel that this development has changed society?

Fewer people are changing residence within the cities and districts. It seems the population has developed a certain relationship to the cows. At the same time, the concept continues to develop: there are new cows and new tasks, districts are changing, and new networks are emerging.

On the health level, we have yet to raise specific data. But we are assuming that the cows' new occupation is having a positive effect on people's stress symptoms.

Would you like to add something else?

We are increasingly seeing that other animals are interested in this model and would like to work with us. Ducks and swans, in particular, have been spotted in the districts taking on more and more tasks, such as accompanying children across the street. The next step will be to assess their needs and coordinate the tasks. I can well imagine that there will be other animals wishing to participate in our social coexistence.

Newspaper: New Delhi Paragraph
Interviewer: Omin

Reading Prohibited

Trends: Open Science, DIY Principle, Selfness

Urs Gaudenz and Patricia Wolf

Extract from the magazine 'Genetic Philosophy' from 04.08.2214:

The notions about the science-based beginning of this millennium are often accompanied by the assumption that it was the era of genetics and genetic engineering. But up until 100 years ago, few people knew their genome, or God's book as it was sometimes called back then, based on my own reading. This was not only because a large portion of society had no access to reading machines that could enable them to decipher their DNA. They were also not capable of reading the genetic code and interpreting the knowledge stored within it. Hence, most had to rely on simple so-called DNA tests, such as 23andMe. Up until the end of the era of the knowledge society, there were periodical bans on reading and interpreting DNA for ordinary citizens. Science was not prepared to lose the monopoly on interpretation.

Although by the end of the second millennium, single parts of the human genome were deciphered and the resulting synthesized proteins identified, however, these analyses were prepared by scientists, which meant: they were not primarily aimed at ordinary people, but at the pharmaceutical industry. This mostly involved selecting genes associated with diseases, so-called genetic defects, the healing of which enabled the pharmaceutical industry to earn a lot of money.

Around 1990, a gene therapy was conducted by doctors of the US Federal Health Institute on a four-year-old girl. The patient Ashanti DeSilva suffered from an immune deficiency and was repeatedly treated with gene therapy. The therapy of Ashanti DeSilva was preceded by a three-year approval process.

As part of the DIY Bio Movement of the first and second centuries of the third millennium, ordinary persons also began to show interest in genetic engineering and, for the first time, they began to openly assert their claims to the right to read them. However, the science community vehemently rejected these claims. In 2004, Steve Kurtz, founding member of the art performance group Critical Art Ensemble, was arrested by the US Federal Bureau of Investigation (FBI) and his lab searched on suspicion of bioterrorism. In 2013, the FBI invited exponents of the DIY Bio Movement with the intention of investigating their motives and to rein them in using a code of ethics. Such ethical codes or also bans on working with genetic material were enforced throughout the entire first century. The bans were always applied restrictively whenever ordinary people claimed their rights to access the genetic code as well as read and interpret it for themselves.

These bans were due to the fact that the movements of that time, which were branded autonomous, and in particular the hackers and nerds, focussed mainly on reading the genetic code and deriving interpretations in order to give laypersons non-scientific access to the human genome. Scientific knowledge was primarily sold to ordinary people through new products and thus embedded in a commercial context that highlighted science's prerogative of interpretation.

Initial efforts to achieve a complete translation of the human genetic code can be found in the middle of the first century within the Hackteria movement. In addition, several lay interpretations emerged throughout all of Europe and their authors explored the entire human genome, including epigenetics. On several occasions, the first century was hence called "the century of the layman's genome". Most of the translators remained anonymous for fear of persecution by the pharmaceutical industry. The numerous violations of the genetic engineering laws show to what extent interested lay persons had already emancipated themselves from the established social views and had asserted their own interpretation claims.

The most significant translation of the first century came from a Swiss man whose name remains unknown. In his preface, he wrote that many simple-minded laypersons far more accurately understood the divine code than any number of scientists. Because even though scientists had been claiming that only they understood science, the reality was that they had never actually given it much attention. Scientists thus feared that people might notice their errors and dreaded the loss of credit and distinction if non-scientists were able to read the genetic code themselves.

The Future Forum Lucerne 2040 'Gencode Revisited' revealed that the first translations had created an impact already a century before their official recognition. Not coincidently, the organisers thus regarded themselves as the successors of the generation "We have always been biohackers", to whom we are indebted for the right to free interpretation of the genetic code.

"Wow", she said, "that's what you get when you transcribe the biblical story of Luther on the reading of the genetic code?" He simply grinned and nodded.

LAST CELEBRATION OF THE MEETINGS

TRENDS: FEMALE EDUCATION WINNERS, SHARENESS, TALENTISM

JULIE HARBOE

The speech uses terminology of the period that has been only slightly adapted for preLife readers in the hope that you can hear us via reverseSpeak.

Dear honoured coThinks,

We are gathered here today to celebrate the last 'meeting' together in this hall. Our European Quality Ministry, as we all know, now has more than 800 units (with the green, yellow and red partUnits). Our periMeter is the safest of the squares. For those among us who are younger, the celebration may not be as exciting as it is for those of us who have known models of bureaucracy and hourly labour, desks, project plans and work processes and work spaces. Back then, it was not the celebrative aliveNess that it is today, and our coThinks, as you have mentioned, had 'structured' units for what was then called Time and Work. For them, meetings were very important.

It is sublimely amazing for me to remember how it was when I first came here to the levels. In the morning, we went into an edifice, sat down at tables and began to write to each other so-called emails using viaCom. From time to time, we could spend up to 3x60 moments of the best morningAir-Life writing. We even wrote back and forth to each other, what we today simply coConnect. This type of coThink organisation by means of the written word was highly respected, up until Randapuri Harensdarab's remarks about the destruction of vibrations via surfacility completely transformed our views on conTextualites.

Part of the Work-Space 'Structure' were the Meeting Rooms. These were somewhat similar to our connectRooms but with essential extraneousObjects, such as tables and coPlants. Because there is so little of this meeting-sprit left – as my grandmother had once said, as far as I know – we have decided to reNovate one such example just for you. Afterwards, and this perhaps may be the most important thing for those of us who have passed a large part of our aliveNess in the Unit-of-Rules and most of our time in the unThink void, we shall give our hearts to peace and release the meetings eternally into the galactic.

As a preLife coThink, I explore the major differEnces we have gone through as a lifeForm. And I think for example of the death of all the horses many, many blossoms ago, that made other forms of human transMission possible, starting with, for example, cars, (which at first were even operated like horses, ha ha).

It is clear to me that this Loss of conNection to the animals, that for so many units were a part of their aliveNess, led to so much more emptiness and coldness than the coThinks have generally understood. The sadNess of the people, the many depressed dogs that later in the following cenTuries caused so much horror on the greyContinents, must be viewed in this conText.

It was a different matter with the meetings, but if we decide today to catapult them into the galaxies, we are very pleased that they will be darkened forever. As with other matters considered normal for the past system – to revert to that old bureaucratic word – it is rather difficult to reNovate the true opinion about the meetings. I still know the very inelegant terminology my grandmother used to describe the meetings: shaking penises (she spoke in the Insular and I believe she called it the Penis Shake). I must admit that I do not quite know how much of this is madThink. For our unit, my grandmother was not only against the unThink, she was an ardent freeThink, but she had stored a lot of Think from the preLife. So according to her, the meetings were designed to give the Masculinum in particular the opportunity to stimulate its role and dominance. This type of interaction was so alien to the Femininum that they distanced themselves from it and identified it as a form of unSpeech rule that is unknown to the Femininum. It seems that arguments were adjusted back and forth until a winner was found.

Because of this game, the Penis Shake, meetings were hence important for the Masculinum – and thus the most famous artwork of the green partUnit is also the Urinal by R. Mutt.

Personally, I find it interesting that today we regard it as an endearing quality that the Masculinum could submit their physical atTention in the bureaucracy in this almost naive way. Of course, the Femininum could also indulge in these irrelevant gestures, and were here especially vitriolic, but my grandmother would prefer not to admit that. Indeed, she belongs to the fierce fourthGeneration feminists and (and this I say with some pride) was very militant, although she later invested many of her valueUnits in the Big Arms Melt.

In meetings you could keep the agendas rolling, as the curators said. As per a typical late definition of the green partUnit, the meetings were the key conTainers for powerFaking. What I always found fascinating as a MASHUP-person of the yellow partUnit was the seriousness with which the Greens were absorbed in their agendas.

The key to the perMutation of the meetings and the reason that they, like the bureaucracy, finally disappeared was, as I have already mentioned, connected with the apPearance of Harensdarap. Harensdarap identified that meetings were a comBination of the strongest surfacility factors for

Think, which led to an almost total enTropy of the conTent. Not only did the persons sit around a table without moving – the highest on the Energy-Loss scale. They also voluntarily followed the written agendas and had a singleBrain defined platform. The apparentPower that was developed here and the total abSence of lifeThink led to the so-called one-way logic, that in the end clogged up Think on the greyContinents and led to the brief takeOver of danceLogic until the colorMinistries finally eMerged. It is surprising that meetings, even though they were not really dePloyment, had survived these transFormations like an invisible force.

Although this briefly weighed heavily on our hearts, the legacy of the meetings gives us a picture of how far we have come since the preLife. No one today would ever think that by sitting around a table, they could stop Think and that the slow one-after-the-other-speech wordChains could lead to a growth in vibrationExchange. The greyContinents had many such strange conTainers. We have only a few of these left and we are happy to bid farewell to meetings. And now we ask, in conSultation with the other continental ministries, the colourful coThink FloraLupa to release the totalcontinentalFolder on meetings forever into the infinite galaxies.

The Annual Brainwash

Trends: Education Business, Female Leadership, Feedback Society

Ute Klotz

Two days ago, Linda and Florence, two professors at the Academy for Future Studies in Bad Berghausen, had yet another significant shift in their views on the state of the world and politics. Linda, a doctorate blogger, and Florence, a doctorate media artist, considered themselves astutely discerning, crisis-tested, and equitable. They shared only one principle, namely, never to be naive. For over 10 years, they had worked at the Academy for Future Studies and, in that time, had experienced a change in the education system that they would not have thought possible. They were now both 39 years old and as of next year would get the title of 'Lecturer with Special Duties'. They were deprived of their professorship for reasons of age. This meant that they would no longer hold the lectures, but only prepare the content.

Their reasoning behind this was that the academy no longer wanted to expose the student women and men to professors of this age. The academy had conducted its own research project on the matter and discovered that students taught by professors of that age experienced enormous anxiety about the future. Moreover, students often experienced recurring periods of eye watering episodes and their parents thus assumed that their children would eventually suffer permanent eye damage as a result. However, the decisive argument, and completely independent of the research results, was that the parents had threated to stop all financial support for their children in the future or to transfer them to another university if the academy administration did not finally take action to deal with this situation. The parents namely believed that their children had to live in a world without disease, poverty or aging for as long as possible. The academy administration then submitted the parents' threats to the leadership cockpit, called TRSS (Totalitarian Rectors Support System), played out a few future scenarios, and then published the TRSS issued regulations via video message. Yes, this was just one of the many significant changes in the higher education landscape in Switzerland.

Two days ago, they had their annual professors' meeting – a mandatory event that all the professors were expected to attend. And so it became a sort of annual ritual to meet prior to the event and recall the highlights of past meetings over coffee. Stories ranged from drunk professors holding their presentations with open flies, to colleagues who had paid others to stand in for them, to members of the academy's management being hurled with eggs, tomatoes and homemade chocolate cream because of their speeches and proposals.

But this was 2020 and the good times were gone. For years now, Linda and Florence have been calling this professors' meeting "the annual brainwash". Because essentially that's what it was: to make clear to the professors, in ways reminiscent of a sect, what they are expected to achieve in order to earn their membership in the Professors' Club. Until now, Linda and Florence had always thought that they met for "the annual brainwash" in Bad Berghausen to regain a bit of body-mind balance: go for an evening swim in the thermal baths, enjoy a relaxation massage, or an evening stroll through the old city. But no, they now knew that this was not the reason or the aim. And of course they had always walked past the Science Fiction Museum, perhaps even had time to visit an exhibition or at least read the posters. But only two days ago, they discovered there was much more to it than that.

On the morning of the annual professors' meeting, everything was as usual. Everyone arrived, alone or in small groups. Some were tired, others tactically put on a cramped smile, and a few brave ones openly revealed how they truly felt: bored and angry. Linda and Florence are tired, but they make an effort to make an expressionless face. They walk through a face scanner, and get an update on the chip under the skin of their palms, which then allows them to read the entire program on the palm of their hands. But first they walk over to the breakfast buffet.

They briefly check the program to find out what is expected of them. Over the past years, the program has increasingly taken the semblance of a script. It states precisely when and how long they're expected to clap, who is expected to cheer or shout out whatever, who should ask a question and who under no circumstances shouldn't, and many more instructions of the sort. Linda and Florence remember that the rector Gisela has been responsible for perfecting this program for the past two years. Gisela, 32 years old, slim, energetic, self-confident and always immaculately dressed. She speaks seven languages fluently, has two PhDs and a Post Doctorate. Since becoming rector, she has delivered one perfect speech after another. Her predecessors were quite the opposite. Yes, after two years we were all still quite impressed by her. And she is admired, even idolised, by many. No one can work more than her. No one can solve complex problems faster than her. No one has a more prefect family than hers.

And today is not different. Gisela captivates everyone with her very beautiful voice as she opens the annual brainwash. Linda and Florence are utterly mesmerised by her when something unexpected happens. Gisela begins to stutter, repeats her sentences, and then falls silent. She stands frozen on the podium. Dead silence fills the hall. Linda and Florence don't dare to look at each other. They simply wait in the hopes that Gisela would start speaking again. But nothing comes.

Instead they hear an unfamiliar male voice over the loudspeaker, "I am the spokesman of an anonymous hacker group. We wish to inform you that Gisela is an android and has always been one. We have deleted her program so that you can finally wake up. Two years ago, the Federal Council decided to deploy the androids, which were created in the nearby Science Fiction Museum, in real life without informing those affected. All the rectors in all the Swiss universities are androids! Be aware... and...". After that all they heard was white noise and the voice was gone.

In retrospect, no one quite remembers exactly how they got home, or what else was said. Linda and Florence, who always thought of themselves as astute, even suspicious, had been assessed for the past two years by an android, a half machine. They were simply stunned. How naïve they had been to have admired a machine. They had spent the past two years as guinea pigs and were constantly being watched. Now, two days later, they still couldn't quite fathom this incredible situation. The Federal Council has so far made no official statement. Gisela's deputy has taken over the position of rector ad interim. And no, they don't know if he's an android. How can they? How are they supposed to know what an android looks like and how to recognize one? And who do they turn to in such a case?

RECLAIMING THE CITY

TRENDS: CLEVER KIDS, DIY PRINCIPLE, SOCIAL NETWORKS

CHRISTIAN LARS SCHUCHERT, UTE KLOTZ AND PATRICIA WOLF

He finally did it. The journey was arduous and the preparation was long and time-consuming. But his friends pitched in, worked with him, and recently pulled an all-nighter. Finally do something, make something, use something. Use his hands not just to prop up his head on the desk, but for what they're actually made for. To grip tools and carry materials, to pat on backs, to draw and gesture wildly. And of course to eat, that ancient ritual of community, to live and let live, and together feel free and alive.

They've been planning it for a long time, to return to the city from their assigned youth employment zones. To reclaim their neighbourhood. And now the time had come. In this moment, at 3:16, they had to give it their all. The 412 small yellow benches they produced last week in rapid assembly line speed had to be placed at the grey square in front of Zuger Stadium as quickly as possible. It took them 3 minutes to build one bench and the 10 friends had set 10 minutes to position them all.

Take one last deep breath, lift the tarpaulin, unload and go. The game began…

As later the video surveillance cameras showed, it took the the boys and girls exactly 8 minutes and 47 seconds. In that time, a wave of pale yellow islands, geometric patterns, and wild chaos spilled all over the square until it was almost entirely concealed under a sea of more than 400 rectangles. Their pictures spread across the social networks like wild fire. They waited.

The first cyclist came after 17 minutes. Within a short period, you could no longer see the yellow of the benches. The first police car drove by around 4:30. The officer looked out suspiciously but didn't dare to get out of the car. Then another police car showed up – by that point the streets were packed with young people. "The tools of creation are the means of impact", he thought. "And to think that only yesterday the mayor had stated on television that it would take years to change the city's spatial planning …"

LILEA'S REPORTS

TRENDS: SMART BUILDING, SHARENESS, REAL DIGITAL

EIN GESCHENK VON CHRIS EBBERT (NOTTINGHAM TRENT UNIVERSITY) AN DAS CREALAB

In 2187, a number of genetically modified animals from a research laboratory in Papua New Guinea escaped gleefully into the jungle, never to return. The insurance companies eventually wrote them off, and by the time Papua New Guinea was restructured into a human free nature reserve in 2201, the incident had been entirely forgotten.

Except by the escaped animals, who had taken charge of their destiny as soon as they had escaped to freedom, and decided to create their own version of civilization, modelled on the human one. Such had been their genetic modification, and they lost no time and established a well-functioning group hierarchy, led by the orang-utans, to realize the vision.

By 2312, the animals had managed to capture a small number of the many thousands of robotic, solar powered clean-up buoys that trawled the oceans of the world on a mission to eliminate all the plastic particles left behind by the mindless civilizations of the 20th and 21st centuries. These unmanned buoys were about the size of small houses, and went their way laser-sintering plastic particles together into big lumps which eventually sank to the ocean floor in large, solid chunks and were thus removed permanently from the food chain of the ocean world. Every now and then, these buoys would wash ashore on some beach, and then eventually get shoved back into the ocean by coast guards or well-meaning citizens to be swept away to continue their work.

Lilea was one of the many genetically modified cats the Papua New Guinean orang-utans employed as spies. She had inherited many remarkable traits from her ancestors, who had broken out of the original research laboratory; her most developed ability was to understand technology and transmit data using WiFi compatible brain waves naturally – she was able to go online and send sound, text, and imagery, simply using her brain. In 2322, she embarked on a hero voyage on one of the captured clean-up buoys on a mission to land in human-populated territory, and send home regular reports on what she saw and learnt from the humans, to help facilitate the imitation of human-style civilization by monkeys in Papua New Guinea.

The crossing from Papua New Guinea to a foreign shore aboard the buoy took many months, and Lilea sometimes feared she would never reach dry land. But she knew the probability to drift ashore somewhere in nearby Australia, or New Zealand, or, if things went less well, Japan or China within six months was high. The buoys were driven entirely by winds and ocean currents, which made sense, considering that those were also the dynamics of the large fields of floating plastic garbage they were cleaning up.

Eventually, Lilea's natural geo-positioning system, which was much like a 21st century GPS, but inside her brain, began signalling to her that the coast of New Zealand was getting closer and closer. The buoy then ended up drifting all along the west coast, down towards the Antarctic, surrounded the southern tip of the country, and started drifting back up with the winds and the currents. The east coast of New Zealand had many bays and peninsulas, and Lilea was almost sure one of these would bring her journey to an end soon. Then, she would be able to leave behind the boring food made by the synthetic protein generator the monkeys had equipped the buoy with, and she would be able to climb out of the interior and hop onto a sandy beach, or rocky cliffs, whichever they might be. She had kept herself fit with the help of a thoughtfully provided climbing tree and scratch post made from self-rejuvenating nylon fibre, which the monkeys routinely installed in all cat buoys doing hero voyages in the name of Papua Orang-Utania.

The great day eventually arrived in the morning of December 15, 2322. With a surprisingly loud crunching noise, the buoy ran ashore on sandy Allans Beach,

Otago Peninsula, New Zealand, a stronghold of yellow-eyed penguins and sea lions only a few kilometres north of the city of Dunedin. The sun was only just coming up on the horizon line, and a few lazy sea lions noticed the buoy and its blinking, red lights, but took no further interest. Penguins were waddling down the dunes and into the ocean, as if going to work, past the large buoy. It looked like nothing they had seen before, but it might have been simply an orange rock, as far as they were concerned.

Lilea knew not to lose any time, as any wave might have swept the buoy back into the ocean. She pushed the big, red exit button; a hermetically sealed hatch blew open with a hydraulic hissing noise, and she jumped out. The hatch would reseal within 12 minutes, so as not to raise any suspicions in passing humans. It would then be just like any other beached clean-up buoy.

A few days later, sheep farmers Mr and Mrs Trellis of Highcliff Road, Dunedin adopted a very pretty cat that had one day simply appeared on their doorstep, as their house cat. They had no idea that Lilea was a Papua Orang-Utanian spy, on a mission to understand human civilization in the year 2322 with all its advancements, and transmit back any insights and observations she might make while living with humans.

The following are transcript excerpts from Lilea's transmissions to her orang-utan mission handler.

December 18, 2322.

I'm in. I approached a human dwelling, acted interested, and was promptly given full admission to the dwelling. The humans seem friendly, and are lavishing me with a lot of attention. It appears that they have previous experience with cats. They did not seem frightened to see me.

Already, I can confirm that most of the images of human dwellings we have been viewing through natural web in past decades are somewhat realistic, while the older archived data from the late 22nd century are definitely now obsolete. I am hereby providing a full description of a human dwelling in 24th century New Zealand:

The structure resembles what 21st century sources used to refer to as an "Earthship". It is barely visible from the outside. The only features drawing attention to the fact that a living space is hidden under the grassy hills are a rather pretty, colourful door with apparently handmade hinges, and several elegant, polished metal window frames of somewhat gothic shape which do not, however, feature any glass. They appear to be mere openings, and keeping out wind and insects is accomplished through an electromagnetic field exuded by the window frames. It appears possible for certain humans to reach and walk through these without any problems, but I can't seem to make the passage, and have to use a small door in the house's main entrance door, which is about cat sized. It appears that biological coding of some kind restricts who is authorized to make the passage through the electromagnetic fields.

The fields appear to present a dense enough air barrier to keep out the often low night temperatures outside, and allow for the creation of a very different, warm, dry climate inside the house. The energy required for the fields seems to come from wires placed in the grass, which seem to harvest electricity out of the ground.

I have watched sheep trying to gain entry into the house through the openings, but they, too failed. They simply seemed to be stopped by something soft and invisible against which they pressed their noses. That is what happens to me, too when I try.
The humans often venture out, using an airborne contraption which appears out of the sky, then normally hovers next to the colourful entrance door of the dwelling until someone either embarks on a voyage with it, or apparently comes back from one. The humans do not seem to own it, and it seems to act autonomously, appearing only when needed, and leaving again as soon as the passengers have disembarked from it. It visually resembles a jelly fish, has many colourful, glowing lights strewn all over its outside, and is completely silent. It travels at such an

enormous speed that blinking your eyes once can mean to miss its departure and disappearance beyond the horizon entirely.

It is coming back now while I am making this transmission, so I need to stop and act like a normal house cat again to remain unsuspicious. Over and out.

December 21, 2322

I am beginning to understand the systems inside the dwelling better now.

The dwelling is very large. It reaches deep down into the side of the mountain, and its many rooms are gigantic and bright. The air is pleasantly warm and dry, and seems purified and enriched with subtle, natural fragrances. Each room has its own. The ceilings are so high that even a tall human could not possibly touch them, even when standing on furniture. And the ceilings do not seem to consist of dense material, but appear airy and sparkle like water reflections. Although the lighting must be artificial, it appears entirely like natural daylight, and it changes during the day, exactly like outdoor light.

The humans are often congregating in groups, resting on furniture which folds out of the walls as needed, where needed. There are no longer pieces of furniture as we have seen them in images from the 21st and 22nd century.

The humans' food is growing inside the dwelling. They eat fruit and vegetables of a large variety, which grow in corners of rooms.

I am doing what I used to do for food when I lived back home in Papua New Guinea – I catch birds and mice outside. The humans seem to find this quite natural for me to do, and so do I.

There is a swarm of birds settling on the lawn outside just now – I need to go. Over and out.

December 25, 2322

It appears to be a special day of some sort. The humans have been acting strangely elated today, getting together, exchanging gifts. The gifts are all spheres of liquids, and everyone drank from them.

December 26, 2322

Unbelievable changes have come over the humans. They have all grown very muscular and furry, and they are suddenly able to jump as high and as far as tigers. They are going down to the ocean to swim with the sea lions. They are as fast as them in the water. They dig up wild roots and eat them. This seems to make them incredibly pleased. I do not recognize them.

December 31, 2322

The humans have left. I have no idea where they have gone. For a while, I saw some of them outside, swinging in the trees like monkeys, emitting merry sounds. One was eating an apple. I have to say I am surprised. They seem to have abandoned their wonderful civilisation to live like animals. And they seem incredibly happy about it.

January 01, 2323

Everyone is gone. Human civilization seems to have come to a happy end. I am deeply puzzled by this. They have worked so hard only to attain all the natural, physical abilities and attributes of us animals. Is this what they really wanted all along? Did they only build civilization to compensate for their physical inadequacies that kept them from succeeding in nature?

February 28, 2323

Nobody has come back. All humans have become happy creatures in the woods. This is so unexpected. I will wait a while longer. Perhaps they will come back.

September 09, 2323

I suggest to abort the mission. Human civilization has definitely replaced itself by an ability to cope with nature as we animals usually do. I no longer see any value in attaining civilization. See you in Papua New Guinea. Over and out.

IN DUBIO PRO REO / GIVING THE DEFENDANT THE BENEFIT OF THE DOUBT

TRENDS: CORPORATE HEALTH, SOLUTION WORKER, HEALTH MANAGEMENT

CHRISTINE LARBIG

"Quiet please", echoed through the courtroom. The murmur in the hall became quieter.

"Please repeat to this court why you continued to take the pill over a period of three weeks," the judge ordered the defendant. The defendant shuffled slightly back and forth on his STRAP chair and cleared his throat. "Our company president ordered us to do so", repeated the 44-year-old man with dark hair and youthful appearance. His facial expression revealed that he was clearly uncomfortable answering that question. And yet he was convinced that he had done the right thing.

"Were you not able to gauge the consequences of taking that pill beforehand? asked the judge.

"Your honour, as one of the top managers of PUniNesGoo Corporation, with more than 2 million employees worldwide, when you join the company it is your duty to assess the consequences and risks of all decisions. All our actions and decisions are based on this policy", the man replied in a confident tone. Confused, he looked over to the 50 other accused. Faces frozen, they sat cold and motionless on their STRAP chairs, which registered and analysed every move. Any anticipated strong reaction by the person seated immediately triggers a restraining mechanism. A total of 5 women and 45 men in grey and dark brown suits sat still, their eyes blank as if they had been administered a drug that suppressed all facial expression.

"I don't understand why you were unable to foresee the chaos you caused?" the judge asked emphatically. "I can't really say. According to our evaluations, a world governed by rational management based solely on reason would inevitably develop into an ecological and peaceful planet. Violence, poverty and hate go against all human reason. We used rational methods to thoroughly discuss beforehand our analyses of the consequences. We had not taken into consideration a chaos scenario," the defendant replied.

A stone flying through the window disrupted the conversation between the judge and the defendant. Shocked, the courtroom visitors rushed towards the wall to protect themselves against any further possible attacks from the outside. On the streets outside the court building, a mob raged. Screams, police sirens, and the blare of destruction resounded through the air. "Quickly, let down the anti-aggression screens," ordered the judge. A court servant pressed a button. The courtroom was immersed in a soft green light that also reflected to the outside. Relieved, the visitors shuffled quietly back to their seats.

How did the decision come about to add the substance Nilatir 2000 to the food you produce and sell worldwide?", the judge asked the defendant. The man in the dark blue suit began to sweat lightly and a measuring device on the chair indicated that its user was experiencing a slight anxiety. The defendant took a deep breath and replied to the question: "We had tested the substance in food over a period of half a year on a test group of around 100 persons. This showed good results. Our researchers and developers did everything possible to ensure that there would be no side effects when taking Nilatir 2000." The judge pressed a few sensors on his table to access the research results of the test. A voice from the table briefly explained the test procedure in a few short sentences. "Did you not know that the Rikbaktsa tribe is immune to this substance?", the judge asked. "No, we could not have known that beforehand. We occasionally use the tribe for research purposes. But we never registered anything negative," the defendant responded.

"Did you not notice that the Rikbaktsa could no longer bear children?", the judge's tone became sharper. "No, as I said, we tested for half a year. It was not a long-term study. This was approved by the authorities and our company president. And in any case, the birth of children is contrary to reason. We don't need more inhabitants on this planet. We already have 10 billion people, and with our interactive cyber parks, we have created alternatives so that the desire to have children no longer arises. We had thought of everything and our reason decided accordingly," said the man in the dark suit.

In a laboratory a decade earlier ...

"Well, Dr Malcom, we finally did it," the stocky man in the white lab coat said to his colleague standing next to him. "We finally managed to turn off the neurotransmitters and synapses, which enables the dorsolateral prefrontal cortex and thus the mind to dominate all our decisions." The man smiled contentedly.

"I still think Prof Dr. Dr. Dr. Dr.Tashikanon that we should stimulate the orbitofrontal cortex a little more. We should still perform a few more tests with a higher dosage of the substance Sanity X to find out whether a higher level of control of the personal-egotistical behaviour could lead to even better results," admitted the researcher.

"In my opinion, that's entirely unnecessary. We have tested enough and the results are extremely positive.

And you know – time to market!" said the man standing next to her and laughed. "Finally there will be managers in companies who will make purely rational decisions without any sloppy sentimentality. Today's managers must be capable of detecting the factual situation and act on it accordingly. The temporal-spatial structuring of perceptions and well-planned and context-based action and communication as well as the development of objectives must be the basis of all corporate decisions. Can you imagine that in the past, employees were simply asked how they felt in specific situations to find out how to improve their efficiency through spatial atmosphere and team building. All rubbish! That only led to the company investing millions in measures of spatial redesign and reorganization. Employees should simply do what they're told. And this is best done by leading them properly. This pill will change the world for the better," Tashikanon proudly declared.

"So, let's get down to work and start developing the new food additive." The two scientists placed the pill back into the vessel that was to be submitted together with the research reports at the next presidential meeting. Tashikanon walked over to the cabinet. He put his hand on the scanner, thereby locking the cabinet and the files stored within it. For a brief moment, their titles were visible: fear, anxiety, joy, happiness, contempt, disgust, curiosity, hope, disappointment, anticipation, elation and dejection ...

Lisa's House

Trends: Female Leadership, DIY Principle, Smart Building

Christine Larbig

Lisa turned off the path and stood in the middle of a colourful, grass and flower scented field. She closed her eyes, deeply inhaled the fragrance in the air and imagined what it would be like for her to enjoy this place every single day. Her neighbours on the adjoining field kindly waved at her. Everyone was simply happy – here, in this nature in the middle of the city. Not a trace of city noise – only the hum of insects and birdsong broke the prevailing silence. Lisa opened her palm, looked at the seed and smiled with satisfaction: "Yes, here is where I shall plant my house!"

MANIPULATING TIME

TRENDS: SELFNESS, FEMALE EDUCATION WINNERS, LIFE DESIGN

CHRISTINE LARBIG

She inhaled deeply, held her breath and – time stood still.

THE JOB INTERVIEW

TRENDS: TALENTISM, CLEVER KIDS, MULTIGRAPHS

CHRISTINE LARBIG

Ralph XXII took a deep breath. He stood in front of the door that could change his life. He has been preparing for this job for some years now. He absolutely wanted it. He had successfully completed various training and development programs. At age 30, he had now managed to acquire the skills it takes to lead and run a colony on a newly discovered planet outside our solar system. He pressed on the sensor that scanned his finger and identified him as a candidate for the job. On a screen next to the sensor, a pretty young woman, no older than 16, appeared and greeted him: "Thank you, Ralph Montgomery for being on time – if not too early – to the interview. Please come in. You can take off your coat next to the entrance. I will then come and fetch you to show you the waiting room. Your interview starts at 13:34. It's now 13:29." Smiling, the pretty, young face on the screen disappeared. The door opened and a scent of lavender wafted towards him. Like everywhere else in the office, fragrances and atmospheric design elements were used to help inspire employees to new ways of thinking.

"Welcome, Mr Ralph Montgomery." The young, attractive woman from the screen walked towards Ralph and shook his hand. "I am Susan and I've have been working here for six years. I am Dr Legan's assistant. May I ask you to follow me in the waiting room. You still have two minutes," replied the fifteen-year-old. Susan walked ahead and stopped in front of a light-green shimmering room that slowly changed into emerald green. "Please sit down and help yourself to anything from the bar next to the aviary. We will then call you. Please then go subsequently to Room 8. Dr Legan will be already expecting you there. Any questions or requests?" Susan asked the young man in the dark green suit. "No, thank you," Ralph replied, smiling. Susan turned and disappeared through the door.

Ralph looked around and sat down on a chair made of bamboo. "Please get ready for the interview with Dr Legan", a voice sounded softly from a speaker in the waiting room. "10, 9, 8, 7, 6 ...". The countdown signalled to Ralph that he should make his way to the interview.

Ralph stood up and walked over to Room 8. The door opened quietly and the twenty-eight-year old Head of Human Resources welcomed him. "Hello Mr. Ralph Montgomery. Thank you for accepting our invitation to talk. Please do come over here and take a seat." Smiling, the casually dressed young man pointed to the group of seat balloons made of recycled SPME fibres. Dr Legan sat down beside Ralph. "May I ask you to place your right hand on the palm scanner during our talk. This is a device that continuously records and analyses your character. There's nothing to fear. This will not hurt," joked the hiring manager. Ralph smiled sheepishly as he placed his palm on the scanner.

"We have twelve minutes for the interview and I would like to come straight to the point. You have applied for our advertised leadership position for the planet colony Xanon. You have passed the tests for physical strength, authority, improvisation, sense and reason as well mathematics, physics and chemistry, astrology and agriculture, with results ranging from good to very good. We are extremely pleased with this. Congratulations," Dr Legan summarized. "Thank you for the opportunity to perform the tests and for the invitation to the interview," replied Ralph, visibly impressed by the compliment.

As you may know, we have received a total of 54,351 applicants for this job. 53 potential leaders who have completed the test with similar results as yours were invited to an interview. You can consider yourself very lucky. Yes, you can be very proud of your qualifications. In the past, a degree in a specialisation was deemed sufficient. Today – and this you have shown – multiple studies in ten or more areas of knowledge are simply the standard minimum requirement. As a hiring manager, I deal with a lot of young and highly qualified candidates." Dr Legan activated a sensor on the table labelled 'record'. "Now please tell me about the possible decisions you would make as head of the colony Xanon," asked the hiring manager. "Well, I have of course made some thoughts on the matter. I can transmit the summary of my proposals from my finger chip, if you'd like," replied Ralph. "Yes, that would be very good. We can then quickly analyse them right now." Dr Legan nodded in agreement and activated the sensor labelled 'absorb'. The data was transferred and added to the candidate's digital profile.

"Now, to summarise briefly, I would like to start a cooperation with the inhabitants of the planet Walon. They have resources that we lack, such as Balminon for growing extremely resistant plants that produce oxygen to a great extent, thereby eliminating all pollutants from the air. Furthermore, I would build a fleet that allows us to use Gamin – an ecological by-product of agriculture – as a fuel. I've already selected the required developers. I could already hire them by the end of next month. The transfer fee to be paid to the developers' current employers would pay itself off within six months. For the construction of the colony, we could use lunar rock. My analysis showed that the import should be no problem and we could already gather the necessary materials for the construction of atmosphere-enhancing buildings within half a year. I would select the future residents strictly according to the specifications of gender, age groups, professions and psychographic characteristics as well as their plans for the future," explained Ralph proudly as Dr Legan read the measurement results of the character scanner and Ralph's digital elaborations on his screen.

"Very impressive, and very well thought out," responded Dr Legan. "Our time is up in two minutes and I first want to thank you again for the talk. In our opinion, you fulfil above and beyond the profile of Head of Colony. Your qualifications and previous experience in the twelve companies in which you have worked make you a very future-oriented and objective-oriented decision maker, who also has the necessary degree of empathy for people. The latter is very important for us, because you have to deal with people who are experiencing major changes and high pressure. Your character scan shows that you think and act very perceptively and carefully in critical situations. You are not the sort of person who only thinks in concepts and hands out instructions. You can connect with people on their current intellectual and emotional levels. You find solutions together with the people you work with and are willing to take a manageable risk. Trial and experience are two important features of your character. In short: In the past, you would have been described as someone with common sense. But, of course, we no longer say that today. You would have been an ideal Head of Colony for us. However, I regret to inform you that we must reject your application," Dr Legan looked at Ralph: "Unfortunately, you're too old."

SHORT AND SIMPLE

TRENDS: NEW LOCAL, POWER OF PLACE, BIO BOOM

CHRISTINE LARBIG

There it stands brightly lit at the end of the city's former industrial zone. The large letters on the roof of the building offer only a hint to what is taking place inside the post-genetic "factory": 'Everything – And Now!'

"Finally," says the man in the white lab coat and sighs in relief. "There she is – the mother of it all!"

SECRETO

TRENDS: GENDERING, POLYLOVE, AGELESS CONSUMING

CHRISTINE LARBIG

They used to be called bars – today they are transforming emotional worlds or short: secretos. The facilities are rather plain and cold. The atmosphere is kept this way to prevent any conversations. It's all about one thing. The stage is a steel platform, and the changing lights and simple seating lined up around the stage make sure that the one hundred spectators have their full attention on what's happening in front of them.

Also in the Secreto with the melodic name 'A Streetcar Named Desire', attractive and mysterious women no longer dance on a pole, their gestures and movements enticing visitors to indulge in their their own erotic imagination – a world beyond reason and rigid intellectual boundaries.

Back then... you fell into a lustful and intimate sensuous intoxication that no one around you could perceive. A feeling that is unimaginable today – as if you were strapped upside down in a centrifuge, arms and legs stretched out, utterly helpless and at the mercy of the forces. As the speed of the centrifuge rises, a tension from your deepest inner being gradually began to spread throughout your body until it suddenly shifted into a sense of falling. The fall was short and intense. A feeling of relief followed. As if you had just sprung from a ten-meter-high rock and into the warm, invigorating sea. The slight movements of the waves rocked your body gently back and forth until a moment of floating set in. The bars were full of these mysterious vibrations that made the audience rise and fall repeatedly. An inexplicable longing for the wide open sea remained after the dancers' performance. It felt as if it was really happening. Only the smell of sweat and the haze of alcohol betrayed that the body and mind were not in the same place.

Today, in 2070, everything is different. In the secretos, metallic plasma bodies play out the events on a platform. They rise and fall at a height of one to two meters. This up and down movement takes place in a slow swinging rhythm. The bodies are a mixture of human, leopard and snake, that transform their metallic-shiny appearance at regular intervals. Their movements are supple and cautious, but at times fast and sudden – much like a past lovemaking between two people whose inner longing had brought them together.

Eronores, that's what they're called. The bodies are a fiction, and yet they're not. At first sight, you might assume they were robots. But their hypnotic movements might lead you to believe they are higher beings who were created to stimulate the collective amygdala in well-measured impulses.

The stage now turns to the left, changing the perspective on these shiny creatures as they now seemingly open up and begin to split, only to morph again into a new form. An emotional moment of sensuality and innocence begins to spread. The music quietens down. Many of the visitors take a deep breath and then sit back and relax. No pungent smell of body odour and alcohol. Perhaps, after all, this is just fiction?

But the era of boring holograms is long behind us. Gone are the pixel-like projections of creatures and emotionless transmissions of empty words. Gone are the days of goggles that fed our eyes a fake experience artificially generated in the computer world, and instantly disappearing as soon as you took them off.

The light goes on and I look around, somewhat confused. I try to imagine how it was back when there were women and men... I lean back...

ANGEL

TRENDS: WOMANOMICS, POST-CARBON SOCIETY, SOLUTION WORKER

JENS O. MEISSNER

Miller cursed. He got into the habit of cursing. With wholehearted abandon. Here in the dark, black, cold of this stark titanium cell, surrounded by tonnes of water pressure, no one could hear him – if he wanted. But there were times he did want to be heard. Quite often, actually. Especially whenever Hilbert issued one of his shitty directives.

Hilbert was a moron of a supervisor – but he was the supervisor. And he had the last word. But Miller secretly knew that it enraged Hilbert whenever he heard his swearing tirade. Especially when it was about one of his stupid decisions. And this was one of them: Miller was to look for nodules. Manganese nodules. Bullshit. For decades they've been using robots to do that. But today, of all days, he gives Miller the job. And so there he was. In an exosuit, a diving container with moveable arms and leg joints, a 120-kilogram underwater astronaut suit. He stumbles, gets saved by the stabilization nozzles, and then is served one of Angel's sneering remarks. As his co-pilot, she sat inside the Rambler, in charge of the controls. She gave him directions, and told him how to return. And she took care of everything. Angel was pretty in a nondescript sort of way. And she had these insecurities. He had no idea why. She certainly had no reason for it. Whenever Miller was really mad, he swore and cursed loudly enough to make Angel shrink in her seat, red-faced in sheer embarrassment. And foul enough to make Hilbert's blood boil. It was perfect. Strangely, Miller always felt better afterwards. Because he really did like Angel. And because he couldn't stand Hilbert, that pathetic wimp.

Since diving down, Miller hoped that there would be more Angels and less Hilberts around in the future. But the Hilberts of the world remained. And the Angels disappeared. And revolutions were rare. After all, Hilbert commanded the boot – the 'Rambler V'. It carried more than 400 people and was crossing from Wales to Canada. Only Hilbert knew why. Miller, in any case, didn't. His now apparent ignorance set him off again into another cursing rant. Miller had nothing to lose at this point; he was the last of his kind that Hilbert could send down there. All the others were either cowards. Or dead. Or both. The four people who could have done it have all not survived the mission in the past few months. Accidents. But Miller knew what he was doing. And he had balls. And no respect for his superiors, at least not for the Hilberts of the world. But then again that's why he was out here and Hilbert was inside. Probably getting a blow job. Or drinking tea. Whatever. Damn it.

Miller took the scooter, a compact towing machine that could easily pull him down into the deep dark for half a day. He couldn't feel the cold outside. That was a good thing. To do a good job, he needed the cold though. It was easy to do in 4-degree water. Otherwise he would have the heating on, and the four lights, and the infrared viewer in the visor of his helmet. Angel had discussed the course with him, and they had gone through it in the simulator. She told him precisely how far he had to go. Much farther than usual. So Miller knew the way. Angel would then guide him back. It took him three hours to get to the spot he was searching for. Behind a small ridge, near a range of underwater springs that spewed hundreds of degrees of hot water. When he came close to them, Miller saw nothing in the HUD. Everything turned red. Before he could correct it, he was boiling hot. So he avoided going near them. When he got dangerously close again, he used the moment for an extensive tirade. And Angel just had to deal with it. Miller needed it.

Why was he searching anyway? They went down with the Rambler around three years ago. With a huge celebration but no one on dock to bid them farewell. There were four other boats at that time. Meanwhile, there must have been thousands of such vessels out there sharing the deep sea. On board, they had everything a community needed to survive. Technicians, researchers, operating personnel, women, children, seniors, simply everything. But still too little. Regular meetings took place underwater. The vessels were joined together. Each one of them was specialised – exploration, extraction of raw materials, and research, but also for relaxation, vacation, or politics. Above water, there were only remnants left behind. The big cities – empty. Only the largest complexes were sealed off and were still habitable for a short while. Those who remained outside collapsed in the heat. Nature was now a desert. Eventually, the balance tipped. Slowly at first, then faster. The sea level rose, countries flooded, others became deserts. Although people could still survive in the cities, eventually they began to look for alternatives. Escaping into space was too expensive and offered no prospects. Water was the solution. Though the ice at the poles was almost gone, the water was still there. For the next few hundred years at least. And for the few who could afford it.

Water had everything: oxygen, energy, biomass, food, raw materials. Everything. One only had to cope with the environment – and survive. That had been perfected. While the first containment vessels could only manage a shallow descent, the 'Rambler V' was a ship of the latest generation. 5,000 metres were not a problem. It was dark everywhere, and the systems were able to derive the necessary materials from any ocean depth. Only sometimes did people still have to get out and explore things for themselves. Something robots could have done. But this took much longer. And – God only knows why – robots either had an idiosyncratic artificial intelligence and did something other than they were supposed to do, or they simply didn't provide enough "overall visibility". After so many decades of robot development, it was still not possible to get a good all-round observation. Aquanauts were still needed to pick up the small but crucial details. That's why Miller had to be here now. In the middle of the night. Abruptly woken up by idiot Hilbert. Miller hoped that his next resounding curse would mortify Hilbert as much, if not more, than Angel.

He reached the plateau behind the smokers. He glided past a whale skeleton. Sometimes he heard them when they swam in shallower waters. Once, one of them glided past him through the beam of his spotlights. Miller could sense his gaze. Reproachful and contemptuous, Miller felt. Others would have wet themselves. But not him. He admired these creatures. It triggered a magnificent swearing rant. Angel heard it. But she was frightened. This time she was the coward. And he let her know that. Angel no longer responded.

Hilbert snapped him out of his thoughts and ordered him to search quickly. He wanted some answers by tomorrow morning. Miller retorted sharply – then silence. More gliding, manoeuvring, searching.

Nothing. Everything cleared. Someone must have already harvested this place. But then, the harvested sites were registered on the map. And Angel knew that. Miller turned back, when he registered a flicker on the screen. The scooter's battery suddenly indicated only 15%, not enough to even get close to the Rambler. "What the hell ...?", snapped Miller. "Angel, what's going on?" Murky blackness moved before his eyes. "Angel?", he yelled in a shrill voice into the microphone. Angel answered, "Miller – no more cursing." The tone of her voice sent shivers down his spine. "What the...? What?", he gasped. "It's too late to apologise for all your humiliations...", she purred, "...now you're going to pay, just like the others." Horror began to rise in Miller. "I want to talk Hilbert immediately. Get him on the microphone – right now!", Miller barked frantically, cursing so much that Angel would have instantly died of shame. She answered – one last time. "Hilbert can't hear you, Miller. Nobody can hear you anymore. Take care!" A crackling in the helmet. Then silence. 11% left. And blackness and cold and smokers. Damn it!

Healthy Flavours

Trends: Downaging, Ambient-Assisted-Living and Health management

Stijn Ossevoort

People say that I'm over-concerned about my health, frankly I don't mind, most people reach the respectable age of one 100 whilst the human body could easily last another 20 years. It's a matter of staying in good shape, which is my mission. I happily spend an hour on my morning ritual to be sure everything is ok. Today is no exception; I just had a long cleansing shower, which I really needed after yesterday.

What a day, it was a whopping 38 degrees, our clothes were sticking to our skin so we couldn't resist going for a swim in the lake nearby. Together with my great grandchildren, Judy and Kevin we spent hours in the water. We had a short ballet contest to see who could perform the most elegant tricks in and under the water. Great fun, but the murky water ended up in my nose and ears.

Ah, I shouldn't forget to check my skin in front of my body scanner, the powerful sun might have caused some abnormalities to the few spots I have on my skin. Although I did use sunscreen but I can never be sure enough. My body scanner is basically a large mirror that takes pictures of my skin and lets me know when there are some health issues, it not only checks my skin but also fat tissues and even my posture. Let's see, everything is ok – a sigh of relief.

I had such a great day with the kids. After the swim I treated them by visiting our local ice-cream shop, called Moodz. The shop has too many flavours to choose from so they actually analyse your feelings and suggest the 10 flavours that best suit your mood. Some amazing technology, a robot servant engages you in a short conversation and combines the answers and the tone of your voice to produce the ultimate mix of flavours. Not sure what mood I was in but the flavours were, lemon, mint, eucalyptus, pine, Aloe Vera, lavender, soap, mouthwash, chlorine and sulphuric acid.

Talking of technology, I've invested in the latest state-of-the-art gadgetry and even had a new room built since our bathroom wasn't big enough anymore. I call it "Uncle Bob's cabin", the absolute feeling of freedom. I'm the proud owner of a breath analyser, which can detect any kind of cancers, diseases and even food-related problems. I also have an ear pincher, nose scraper, sweat analyser, an atomic resonance scanner and a laser-shaving device, which can even implant hair.

Let's not forget to brush my teeth, nothing to worry about on this end. I have my little helpers, who will do the job for me. I'm very pleased with my latest addition, the Dent-o-ants. Life is bliss; I just have to pour the robot ants into my mouth and wait a few minutes whilst my little friends do the job.

Ahh, yesterday, what a lovely day, after having our ice creams we played football in the park until it was dark. What a bummer, Kevin managed to step right into some nasty dog mess. How angry I was, although it wasn't his fault, but I made sure he cleaned his shoes. "How should I clean them?" he pathetically asked – "I can't be bothered as long as they are as good as new again", I replied. He later assured me that he had found some little helpers.

Mmm, where does the extraordinary taste come from?

MATRIX MULTIPLICATION

TRENDS: EDUCATION BUSINESS, 24/7 SOCIETY, REAL DIGITAL

ROLAND PORTMANN AND PATRICIA WOLF

Alma van Dyck gazed out into the Antwerp rain. She was bored. Damn these robo coachings! Nothing could be less interesting, but the Lucerne University of Applied Sciences and Arts was renowned worldwide for the high quality of its robot-assisted teaching. Every single student was given a robot that provided them with teaching content – no matter where they were. This brought enormous savings in terms of human teachers and simultaneously attracted high numbers of students. That's why, week after week, every Sunday night at seven o'clock, she was in the virtual meeting room, where she stared at the blank faces of the instructional robos, and every single time she asked herself why she was there. Mathematics was simply mathematics, and in the last 5 years, there had been only minor changes in the courses 218-220. These chapters dealt with matrix multiplication.

Alma sighed, then started the virtual meeting room. The figures of 10,000 instructional robos appeared in 3D space. Alma opened the coaching by asking the usual question: "What is your feedback on exceptional events in the classroom for matrix multiplication?" Instructional Robo 319 sent an attention message and appeared magnified in 3D space. Alma was surprised – there had never been any feedback on matrix multiplication. "My student has had difficulty understanding why one had to be able to multiply matrices. He refused, pointing out that for the past 20 years his computer can do this much faster. I wanted to ask if this is just a phenomenon that occurs in humanoids from Africa, or whether it happens on other continents as well?"

A short flickering in the virtual space showed that the system was briefly overloaded. After 19 seconds the Turbo Analyser displayed the summary of responses from 6472 instructional robos on the big screen. 93.5% of the respondents had similar experiences and proposed that from now on they should only focus in the class on the applications of matrix multiplication and no longer on actually multiplying matrices.

Alma found the proposal reasonable. It was certainly in line with the University of Lucerne's strategy, which in the last 15 years has shifted the focus more on practical application than on basic knowledge. Her boss would credit her performance account for this new feature with at least 10 rationalization points. "Good," she said, "then that's what we'll do. Are there any more extraordinary events to report?" After no further messages were registered from the instructional robos, she closed the session and climbed out of the bathtub. The water was getting cold.

In the secret Robot World Domination Headquarters in Alaska, a new message came in. After correlating with the reports from other universities, on the list titled "Things people can still do without robots in 10 years", the entry 'Matrix Multiplication' was deleted.

Bedtime Story From The Future I

Trends: Slow Mobility, Life Force, Permanent Beta

Christian Lars Schuchert

The Future is a Hedgehog

She had risen too late.
The morning sun now filled the entire room.
So tired she was, though she had not even run.
She shook off the sleep from her quills.
Outside, dead as a doornail, lay the hare.

+++

BEDTIME STORY FROM THE FUTURE II

*TRENDS: MOBILITY, SMALL-WORLD NETWORKS, POWER
OF PLACE*

CHRISTIAN LARS SCHUCHERT

Have you sawn it? – A parable in simple past future progressive morphology.

It should have had been there yet tomorrow. Together they were will have broken down and wasing chased down the road. No police but very super-fast. Over the edge they sailed and between the corner pocket hole. Silent noise lurked at these. Us was followed. Said the spider to the fly – leg it, I'm coming!

+++

BEDTIME STORY FROM THE FUTURE III

TRENDS: PHASE FAMILIES, LIFE DESIGN, NEW MEN

CHRISTIAN LARS SCHUCHERT

AAC BBC DD EE

Come now – I'm ready for you!
Armed to the teeth, smart, and at all times
steeled for the giant blow.

Because if you can do it all and make it all,
brings us progress and gains you visions.
But, can I wait that long, I wonder?

Oh come now, future, and be mine,
For my will is to always be fine

And follow I shall their call
The ones who say they know it all.

VISITING PAUL

TRENDS: SMART SENIOR SERVICES, HEALTH STYLE, EMPOWERMENT

URSULA SURY

I finally managed to park the personal transport drone in front of the 'Comeback' home for regressive burnout patients. Had I had the new generation drone that you can fold up to the size of a folder by pressing a button, I wouldn't have been this late. I had ordered the Pocket-Pers drone, but because of a virus in the e-Money network, it still hasn't come out of the 3-D printer... It sucks.

I arrive at the entrance of the home, which dates back to the year 2050. The access control technology is just as old. I announce myself via iris scan. Within seconds, the door opens and a friendly voice greets me.

The transmitter brings me to the 596th floor of the Outtimer department. These are patients who can't cope with our highly interactive and networked life. The archaic and one-dimensional interior furnishings and layout of the place never seize to impress me. These patients are simply overwhelmed with our multifunctional living/working/leisure spaces.

I find my former neighbour, Paul, in his room engrossed in his favourite activity: filling out forms and transferring the results to an ancient computer – as today's interactive devices were once called. They found this old program, called SAP, specifically for Paul that he liked to work with. It was evidently complicated, but it helped make him calmer and they could reduce his daily dose of Joy Bringer.

Every time I see him, Paul tells me that he had delivered his SAP reports to his boss on time. Tomorrow, he had a reporting session for which he was now well prepared. But his fear of possible accounting errors had given him many a sleepless night.

Paul has lost touch with our time, as have all the patients in the 'Comeback' home. He still believes in SAP reports, and hierarchical systems with bosses and subordinates. Our quality and content driven modern life with its many interactions confuses him so much that he goes crazy. Yet Paul was once a respected employee in the middle management level of an organization in the healthcare industry.

As a result of general structural changes in the digital transformation, the organization was then released from its classical structure, and the single tasks are now only implemented in cooperation networks. Many people simply could not cope with this kind of social and economic change. That's why we have so many specialised institutions.

I speak with Paul about his reports and his bosses, until we are interrupted by the hybrid therapist. Paul is being picked up. Today he has a one-hour resilience training.

THE FUTURE LIES IN YOUR SLEEP!

TRENDS: VITAL ENERGY, AGELESS CONSUMPTION, QUALITY OF LIFE

MICHAEL DOERK AND PATRICIA WOLF

"That's yet another load of nonsense coming from you! If the university squanders ECTS points on modules that teach the students that they must be constantly designing the future, when and with what outlook will they be released into the present?"

Dr B. thought for a moment. "A future without a past is not possible. If I make students design the future, they will always do so in reference to their own past and present. Future design is as such always inherently present design."

The questioner stretched up for attention. "But what kind of a present is this if we're constantly busy trying to shape the future instead of allowing the future to just happen through our present actions? That ultimately means that we spend our entire time in the present already anticipating the future! Not to mention the past that arises from it!" he complained.

"But my dear sir, that really isn't how it is. We live our real lives and we also need the future – because where else would we get our goals, dreams and motivation to go our own way and better the world," she responded calmly, trying to de-escalate the situation.

"Exactly. You said it, dreams. When we dream at night, during the cyclic association and dissociation processes, compression, decompression, and consolidation of the present and the past continuously take place, thereby generating visions of the future. But, seriously, who today gets enough good sleep?", argued the man from the audience triumphantly. "I do!" replied Dr B.

"We'd still have to check that, but if we set aside your particular case, the statistics tell a different story," he countered. "Sleep deprivation is currently one of the most significant social phenomena. People no longer use the potential of sleep to naturally shape their visions and future. Instead, they attempt to keep everything under control, at least in the medium term, by using business plans, ideation processes, quality and health management, and scheduling apps. We plan more than we really live. We prefer rob ourselves of sleep with absurd activities and then call it living our dreams." The questioner looked over provocatively to Dr B. on the stage, anticipating her reaction.

She cleared her throat. "No, I don't see it quite like that. Of course, promoting and preserving the resource of sleep in order to maintain a natural design of the future in the population is an important social health goal. On the other hand, it requires that we make a qualified investigation of future trends also during our waking hours, so that we can manage to move beyond the capitalist and individualistic tendencies in our society. The future, and we know this from trend studies, belongs to the collective – and we should make conscious steps towards it!" "And that best fully rested!" he interjected as the audience applauded in delighted consent.

The moderator sounded the bell indicating the end of the Q&A session, set up as part of the communal future podium, and the hall lights went on. The participants rose from their seats and streamed into the break zone, engrossed in animated conversations. Dr B. stepped off the stage and walked up to the questioner. "That was an interesting discussion. I would very much like it if we could pick up on this again," she said. The addressed man nodded. "Of course, that would be my pleasure, and by giving you my business card, I will have achieved my current viral marketing and communication goals", he emphasised with a wink.

Confused, Dr B. took his card. Under his name, which was framed by clouds and sheep, there she read emblazoned in big letters: Key Account Manager, Your Bed Shop "The future lies in your sleep."

MENTAL MOVIE

MEGATRENDS: BIG DATA, SELFNESS, SMART SENIOR SERVICES

BARBARA KUMMLER AND PATRICIA WOLF

"Watch out, here comes another schizophrenic with a penchant for porn," he whispered. Silence fell on the control bridge. Everyone looked in anticipation at the screen with the material. After the mobile contacts and travel photos were uploaded, an initial profile emerged. An accurate description of the around 70-year-old man in the observation room, with his faintly distant gaze and sauntering gait.

Dr Wiebke Fröhlich leaned forward. "Shall we try out the swimming pool program?" Stefan Uurs apprehensively shook his head. "Isn't this program intended for incurable cases?", he asked. Dr Fröhlich secretly agreed with him. But perhaps this was a unique opportunity, she thought. The swimming pool program had never been used in their institution before. "I think we should risk it," she said resolutely.

Uurs swallowed. What could he do. She was, after all, his supervisor. Reluctant, he walked to the corner with the control device. "Are you sure?", he asked. Dr Fröhlich nodded. Uurs called up the program. They both stared eagerly at the transmission from the observation room.

The man flinched. His eyes seemed to swell out of their sockets. He didn't move, just like the others from his group. The brain waves on the screen indicated high flight reflexes with a simultaneous paralysis of the locomotor system. Slowly, the group pushed towards the exit. At the door, the man turned around again. He smiled. Dr Fröhlich also smiled.

Minutes later, the man received his shopping from the counter in the museum shop. 'Mona Lisa – A Collage of Swimming Pool Pictures'. He was more than happy to pay 2,900 euros for the perfect illusion for the bedroom. Dr Fröhlich continued to smile.

FSC
www.fsc.org
MIX
Papier aus ver-
antwortungsvollen
Quellen
Paper from
responsible sources
FSC® C105338